WHAT
GRANDPAS
DO BEST

Enjoy!!

In loving memory of my grandparents
—L. N.

In memory of my beloved grandmother
Dorothy Chancellor Currey
—L. M.

WHAT GRANDPAS DO BEST

BY **Laura Numeroff**

ILLUSTRATED BY **Lynn Munsinger**

SIMON & SCHUSTER BOOKS FOR YOUNG READERS
New York London Toronto Sydney Singapore

Grandpas can play hide-and-seek,

make you a hat,

and take you for a walk.

Grandpas can paint with you,

show you their photographs,

and teach you how to dance.

Grandpas can take you on a picnic,

show you some magic tricks,

and help you fly a kite.

Grandpas can take you to the beach,

help you build a sand castle,

and take a nap with you.

Grandpas can play games with you,

give you a bath,

and sing you a lullaby.

But best of all,
Grandpas can give you
lots and lots of love.